2014 OCT

Noah

Methuselah welcomes his
grandson, Noah…

Published by Plough Publishing House
Walden, New York
Robertsbridge, England
Elsmore, Australia
www.plough.com

ISBN: 978-0-87486-639-1
20 19 18 17 16 15 14   1 2 3 4 5 6

Printed in Hong Kong

Noah

A Wordless Picture Book

Mark Ludy

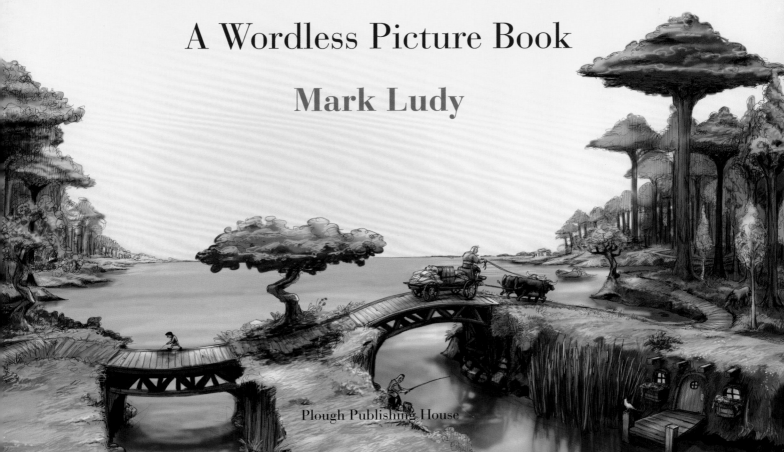

Plough Publishing House

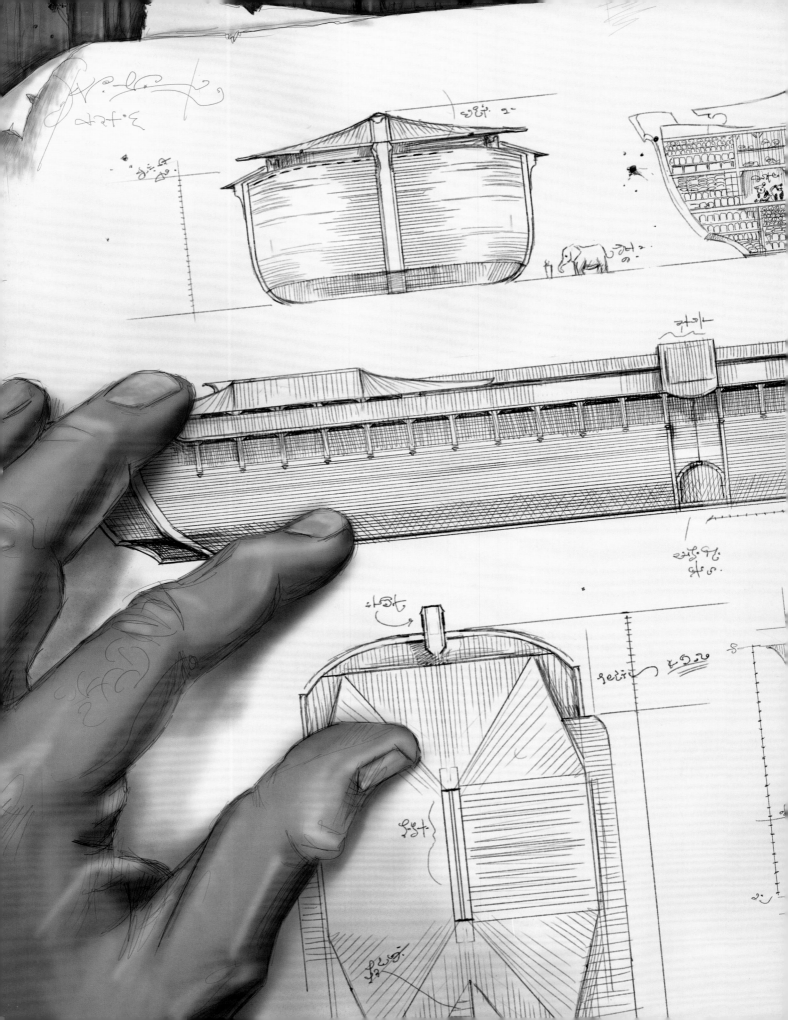

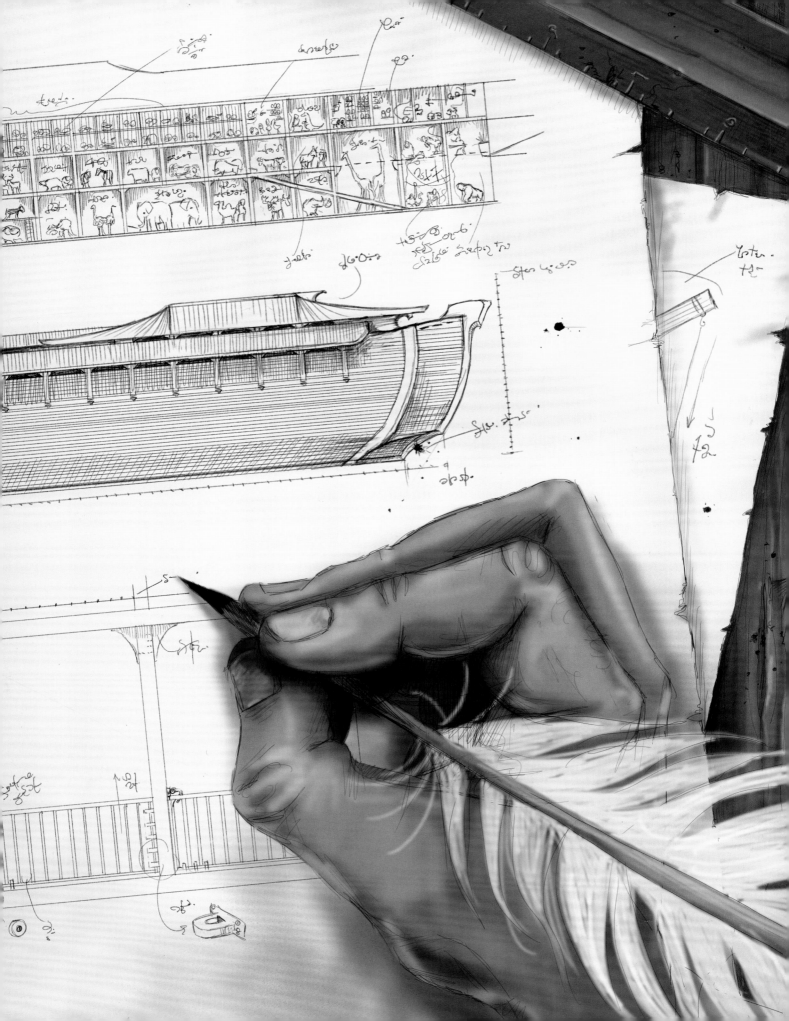

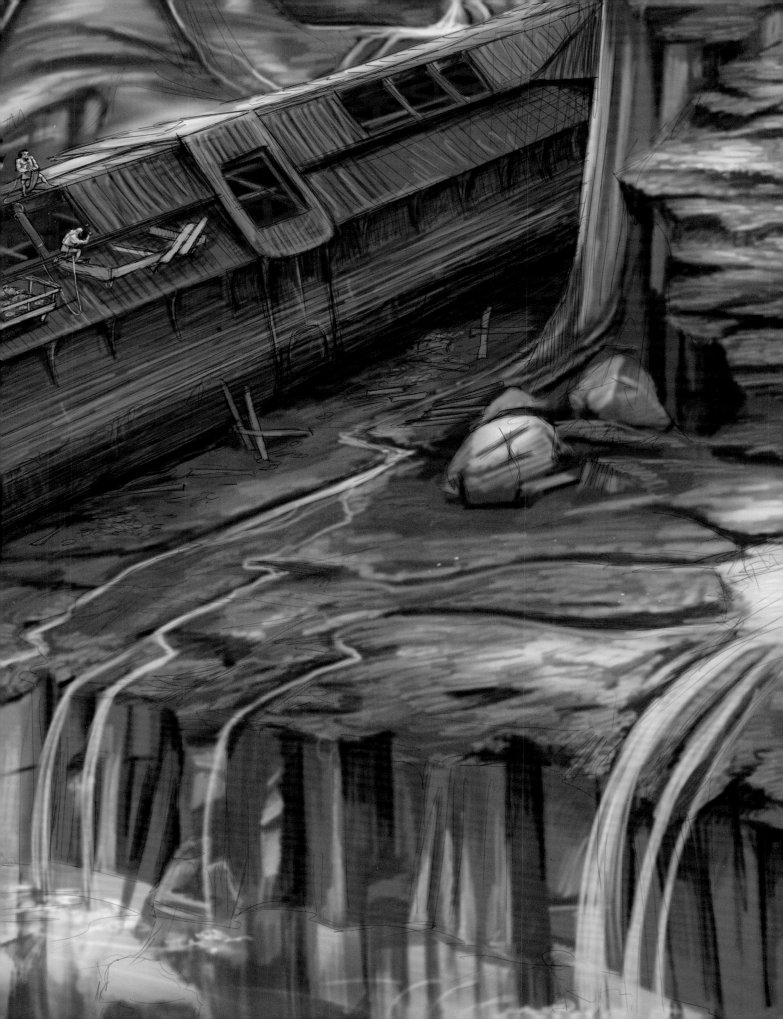